WALT DISNEY'S

MICKEY'S CHRISTMAS CAROL

By Elizabeth Spurr

Illustrations by DRI Artworks

Ebenezer Scrooge hurried past the joyous Christmas carolers, who called to him, "Give a penny for the poor, Gov'nor?"

"Bah, humbug!" Scrooge replied, angrily.

When Scrooge reached his office, he knocked snow from the sign SCROOGE & MARLEY, which Scrooge had still not replaced. Jacob Marley, his partner, had died seven years ago that very evening. He and Scrooge had built a good business robbing widows and swindling the poor.

Inside the office, Scrooge's clerk, Bob Cratchit, shivered as he copied letters. Surely, Scrooge wouldn't mind if he used some coal to heat up the room.

As Bob lifted the scuttle, Scrooge burst into the room. "What are you doing with that piece of coal?" Scrooge cried.

"I was just trying to thaw out the ink," replied Bob.

"Bah! You used a piece last week!" Scrooge said.

As Scrooge sat at his desk, weighing his gold coins, the office door burst open. "Merry Christmas!" his nephew, Fred, cried out, offering his uncle a wreath.

"Christmas?" snorted Scrooge. "Humbug. Keep your wreath. Now, out! Out!"

After Fred had left, Scrooge called to Cratchit. "And I suppose you expect tomorrow off?"

"Why, yes, sir," Cratchit said hopefully.

"Then make sure you come in early the day after!" cried Scrooge.

That night at Scrooge's house, he heard the sound of clanking chains. The ghost of his partner, Jacob Marley, appeared.

"Ebenezer, remember when I was alive, I robbed the widows and swindled the poor?" wailed Marley. "As punishment, I'm forced to carry these heavy chains through eternity. And the same thing will happen to you.

"Tonight, you will be visited by three spirits. Do what they say, or your chains will be heavier than mine." With a clink and clank Marley disappeared.

Later, as Scrooge tried to sleep, a little
cricket appeared in a top hat.

"Who are y-you?" Scrooge asked.

"Why, I am the ghost of Christmas
Past. We're going to visit your past,"
the small creature said, pointing out
the window into the night.

Remembering Marley's warning, Scrooge held on to the tiny creature as it flew out the window and into the darkness. "Whoops, not too tight now!" the ghost yelped, squirming inside Scrooge's clamped fist.

Soaring over snowcapped roofs and winding streets, they landed by a cottage window.

Scrooge looked in the window. He saw his boyhood love, Isabel, dancing with a smiling young man.

"That was you," said the spirit, "before you became consumed by greed."

Then the spirit whisked Scrooge away to another scene that took place ten years later in Scrooge's office. Isabel was crying. Scrooge remembered that he had foreclosed on Isabel's cottage and had lost her forever.

Scrooge lowered his head in sadness. When he opened his eyes, he was back in his own bed!

All of a sudden, Scrooge felt a heavy hand on his shoulder. A fierce voice boomed, "I am the ghost of Christmas Present."

Scrooge looked up and saw a giant peering in through the roof. The huge ghost snatched Scrooge from under the covers and carried him off into the night.

The next thing Scrooge knew, they were in front of Cratchit's shabby house. Through the window he could see the family about to carve a small, scrawny goose. A boy on a crutch hobbled into the room. It was Bob's son, Tiny Tim. "If you don't change your miserly ways, I see an empty chair where Tiny Tim once sat," the spirit said glumly.

The scene shifted to a later time. Scrooge found himself in a foggy grave-yard, facing a hideous dark specter. "Are you the ghost of Christmas Future?" Scrooge asked nervously. But the spirit just pointed to a small grave site where the Cratchits stood sobbing. Scrooge realized that Tiny Tim was dead.

"Tell me these events can yet be changed!" Scrooge pleaded.

The spirit pointed to a deep pit in a deserted part of the cemetery.

"Whose lonely grave is this?" asked Scrooge.

"Why, yours, Ebenezer," replied the spirit, slapping Scrooge on the back.

"Oh, nooo!" Scrooge cried as he tumbled into the now flaming grave. As he fell, he remembered all the people he had wronged. "I'll change! Let me out! Let me . . ."

Scrooge once more awoke in his bed. The sun shone bright; Christmas bells were ringing. "It's Christmas morning!" he cried. "I haven't missed it! The spirits have given me another chance!"

He threw on his hat and coat and dashed outside. "Merry Christmas!" called the people on the street.

"Merry Christmas, to one and all!" Scrooge cried, giving handfuls of gold coins to the folks collecting money for the poor.

Rat-a-tat-tat! Bob Cratchit heard a sharp knock at his door. When he opened it, Scrooge walked in.

"I've brought a bundle of work for you," Scrooge said.

"B-but, sir, it's Christmas Day," said Bob.

Scrooge dropped the sack on the floor. Out fell dozens of presents. He grinned as he watched the children's faces light up with joy.

Then Scrooge offered the family the most wonderful gift of all. "Bob Cratchit," he said, "I'm giving you a raise, and making you my new partner! Merry Christmas!"

Everyone gathered around the table to eat the plump Christmas turkey that Scrooge had brought. How good it feels, Scrooge thought, to be generous and kind.

"God bless us, every one," said Tiny Tim.